MEDIA LITERACY

IDENTIFYING FAKE NEWS

by R. L. Van

BrightPoint Press

San Diego, CA

© 2022 BrightPoint Press
an imprint of ReferencePoint Press, Inc.
Printed in the United States

For more information, contact:
BrightPoint Press
PO Box 27779
San Diego, CA 92198
www.BrightPointPress.com

LIBRARY OF CONGRESS CATALOGING-IN-PUBLICATION DATA

Names: Van, R. L., author.
Title: Identifying fake news / R. L. Van.
Description: San Diego : BrightPoint Press, [2022]. | Series: Media literacy | Includes
    bibliographical references and index. | Audience: Grades 7-9
Identifiers: LCCN 2021009952 (print) | LCCN 2021009953 (eBook) | ISBN 9781678201982
    (hardcover) | ISBN 9781678201999 (eBook)
Subjects: LCSH: Fake news--United States--Juvenile literature. | Media literacy--United
    States--Juvenile literature.
Classification: LCC PN4888.F35 V36 2022 (print) | LCC PN4888.F35 (eBook) | DDC
    070.4/3--dc23
LC record available at https://lccn.loc.gov/2021009952
LC eBook record available at https://lccn.loc.gov/2021009953

CONTENTS

AT A GLANCE

- Fake news has false information. This information can come from stories that are written to trick people. False information can also come from stories accidentally. This happens when journalists make errors. It can also happen when readers share information that was meant as a joke.

- People may create fake news on purpose. They may do it to make money. They may also do it for political reasons.

- Fake news is as old as news itself. It became more widespread as newspapers became easier to print and sell.

- In the 1900s, many news outlets made standards for truth in journalism. But today's technology has made fake news more popular again.

- Fake news can have serious consequences. For example, it may contribute to or spread dangerous

conspiracy theories. Fake news has led people to commit acts of violence.

- There are many helpful ways to identify fake news. Smart media consumers can research claims to see if they're reported by other sources. They can also look at URLs. In addition, they can explore websites.

- People should read and evaluate stories before sharing them. This can help reduce the spread of fake news. They can let friends know if something is inaccurate. If the false information is found on social media, people can report it to the site.

READING FAKE NEWS

Samira and her friend Oliver loved animals. They volunteered together at the local animal shelter. They both wanted to be veterinarians.

One morning, Oliver sent Samira a link to a news article. It was a story he'd seen on Twitter. The headline was in all caps. It said that animals at their local zoo had escaped.

Fake news stories are often intended to grab people's attention.

The main picture showed empty zoo

habitats. There was a video on the page

too. The caption said someone took it on

It can be easy to send fake news articles to friends without realizing it.

their cell phone. It showed a giraffe walking through the streets.

As Samira read, she was surprised to see lots of spelling errors. And she noticed a quote from a zookeeper. The article didn't give his name. The zookeeper said he was glad the animals had escaped. He said that they smelled bad and took too long to feed. Samira thought that was a strange thing for a zookeeper to say.

Samira took a closer look at the site. It seemed like a newspaper's website. But there were lots of ads. She remembered learning about signs of fake news in school. She googled the story about the zoo. No other news stories about it popped up. But a fact-checking website said the story was false. It also said that the photo of the

empty exhibit was from a cleaning day.
And the video of the giraffe was created by
a computer.

Samira texted Oliver back to let him
know. They were both relieved. The animals
were safe. But they wondered how many
people had been fooled by the story.

THE DANGERS OF FAKE NEWS

Samira and Oliver are fictional people
who encountered a fake news story.
But false information is very common in
today's world. Many people worry about
its influence on political issues. Fake
news stories can have real-world effects.

If one person believes a fake news story and another doesn't, it could cause conflict between them.

They can undermine governments. They can make people question free and fair elections. They can even lead to violence. It's important for people to be able to spot fake news. By identifying it, people can avoid letting fake information shape their opinions.

CHAPTER ONE

WHAT IS FAKE NEWS?

F ake news is information that is not true.
Most of the time, fake news refers to

news stories that are made up. They are

written by people who are spreading lies on

purpose. But some false information comes

from people who aren't trying to trick

others. This information is harmful as well.

Anyone can come across fake news stories online.

Understanding the different types of

false information helps readers spot untrue

stories more easily. There are two main

types of false information. These are known as disinformation and misinformation.

DISINFORMATION

Disinformation is false information that is written to mislead people on purpose. This is what is usually meant by the term *fake news*. People may completely make up information. Or they may take real information but intentionally share it out of context. They try to trick people into thinking something happened differently than it truly did. Stories with disinformation are written to spread lies. These stories may

It can be easy to make a website look like a legitimate news source.

be published on websites. The websites are

often designed to look **credible**.

There are a few reasons people create

and spread disinformation. One reason

is to make money. Fake news creators

get money from ads on their websites.

The more people visit a site or click on ads found there, the more money the website makes.

Jestin Coler used to run a fake news business. When he started the business, he was interested in seeing how fake news spread. Coler said, "The whole idea from the start was to . . . publish blatantly or fictional stories and then be able to publicly denounce those stories and point out the fact that they were fiction."[1] But that didn't happen. Many people read the fake stories. They believed them. After a while, Coler started making a lot of money from ads on

Companies buy ads on websites. They hope people will see the ads and buy their products.

the sites. This may have given him a reason to keep running the sites.

People may write fake news for political reasons. Some people want to make the politicians they disagree with look bad. Some may want to help the politicians they like. They may write lies to get people to feel the same way about certain political figures.

In addition, some fake news creators make up stories about major political issues. They want to change people's minds on the issues.

There are many other reasons people may want to create and spread

THE PROBLEM WITH FAKE NEWS

Fake news can cause major problems. When people share fake news, it can hurt their credibility. Their peers might not take their arguments seriously. Students who use it may get bad grades. Fake news can also hurt society. It may influence people's votes. Hateful fake news can lead to violence against certain groups of people. Some fake news can make people distrust credible news sources or the government. It can even lead to violent protests, riots, and terrorist attacks.

disinformation. They may tell lies about a product to try to sell more of it. Businesses may lie about their competitors. Some people may even write stories about others just to be cruel. People with racist, sexist, homophobic, or other hateful beliefs write lies about other groups of people. They want to make others dislike and fear these groups.

MISINFORMATION

Misinformation is false information that wasn't intended as fake news. Stories with misinformation aren't written to trick people. Sometimes false information is published by accident. Other times people believe information that was meant to be a joke. They spread these stories.

Some misinformation comes from poor journalism. News writers may be on tight deadlines. They may believe they need to publish stories even if the facts aren't **verified**. Or they may misunderstand information they are writing about. Reliable news outlets often hire fact-checkers. These people make sure information in news articles is correct. This helps prevent misinformation from getting published.

Journalists may not intend to mislead people, but it sometimes happens.

Misinformation can also come from **satire** or **parody**. These are forms of humorous writing and news reporting. The people writing them don't want to fool people. They are trying to make a point about something, such as society or current events. Or they are simply trying to be funny. But readers might not realize that these stories aren't true. They may share them with others. They present them as fact.

WHAT ISN'T FAKE NEWS?

It is important to recognize that writers and news sources can have certain opinions or political slants without being fake news. Some people don't like news stories that criticize politicians they support. These people might claim the stories are fake. Even the politicians themselves may say this. However, if the facts in a story are accurate, it is not fake news. Opinions can't

Some people have protested against the media. They may believe legitimate news sources create fake news.

be proven or disproven. But facts can. If the information presented as fact in a story is true, even if there are also opinions in the story, it isn't fake news.

HOW FAKE NEWS SPREADS

The creators of fake news use many different methods to spread disinformation.

One is bots. Bots are computer programs. They work on social media platforms. Bots are designed to act like real people. They interact with other users. They share information, such as fake news. Bots spread these pieces to large audiences. In addition, fake news creators might buy advertising space on websites. This helps promote their fake content.

Fake news also spreads through trolls. These are people who purposely create conflict online. They write untrue or unkind things. They may do this just to be mean or to get attention.

SHARING FAKE NEWS ON PURPOSE

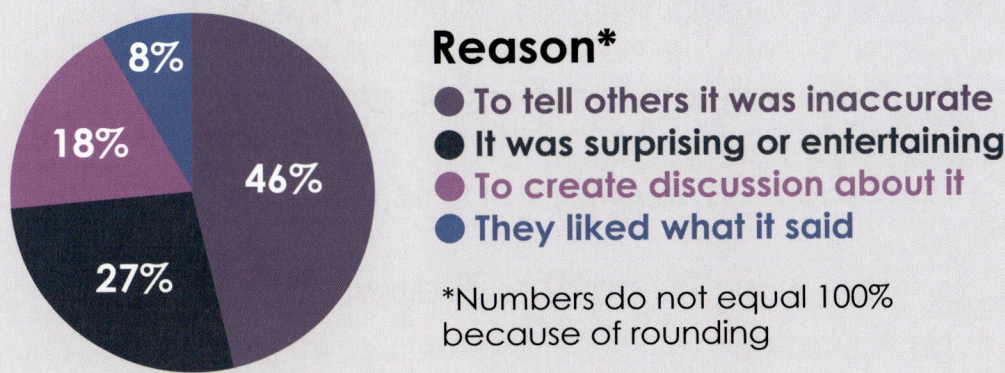

Reason*

- To tell others it was inaccurate
- It was surprising or entertaining
- To create discussion about it
- They liked what it said

*Numbers do not equal 100% because of rounding

8%
18%
46%
27%

Source: Amy Mitchell, et al., "Americans See Made-Up News As a Bigger Problem Than Other Key Issues in the Country," Pew Research Center, June 5, 2019. www.journalism.org.

The Pew Research Center did a poll in March 2019. It asked US adults if they had shared news they knew at the time was fake. Ten percent of US adults said they had. They gave a variety of reasons for doing this.

One of the biggest ways fake news spreads is through everyday people. People fall for fake news stories. They share them on social media. One 2018 study found that

Twitter users are 70 percent more likely to share fake news stories than credible ones. Fake news creators write outrageous stories and headlines. They want to create strong emotional responses in people.

WHY WE FALL FOR FAKE NEWS

People believe fake news for many reasons. They are more likely to believe stories that other people seem to like and believe. This is part of why bots are good at spreading fake news. Also, people may feel social pressure to believe or share a story. Political **biases** also lead people to believe fake news. People are more likely to believe information that lines up with their political views. Fake news stories also bring up emotions in readers. This can include fear and anger. These emotions make readers less able to think clearly.

These emotions make people more likely to believe the stories. Then they share the stories with others. Craig Silverman studies fake news. He described how advertising and emotion help fake news spread. He said, "The false misleading stuff does really well . . . because it's highly emotion-driven. It tells people exactly what they want to hear. It makes them feel very comforted and it gets them to react on the platform. And the platform sees that content does really well and [it] feeds more of it to more people."[2]

CHAPTER TWO

WHAT IS THE HISTORY OF FAKE NEWS?

It may seem like fake news has been around only as long as the internet or social media. But people have been spreading fake news for centuries. Fake news has changed a lot over the years. Some of the fake news today shares similarities with the fake news of the past.

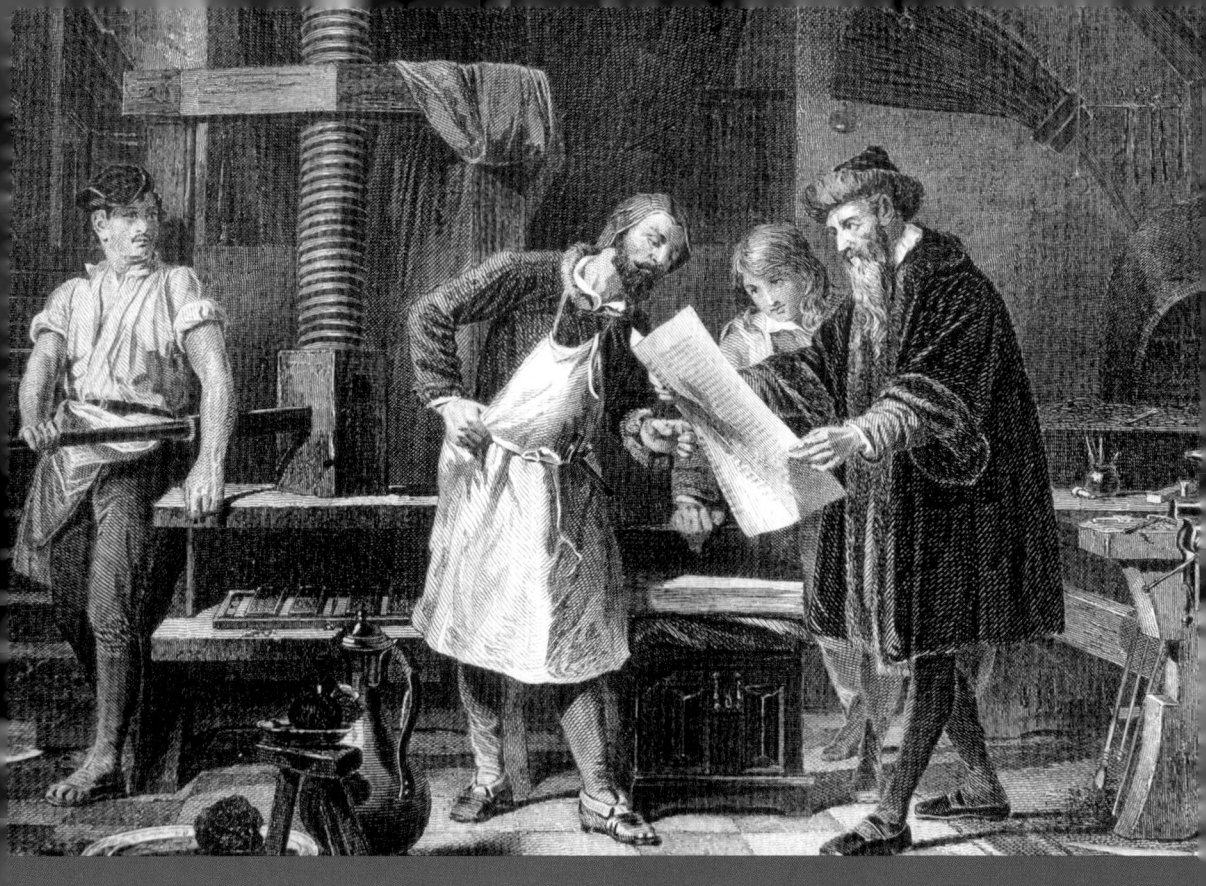

Johannes Gutenberg (right) was from Germany. His printing press gave more people access to books and news.

THE DEVELOPMENT OF FAKE NEWS

The idea of news as we know it today became popular in Europe during the mid-1400s. That's when Johannes Gutenberg introduced the new printing press. This made it possible to print more copies of news stories for people to read.

The information in these news stories was often hard to verify. A lot of news came directly from the government or religious groups. Sometimes religious authorities created fake news. They wanted more people to join their religions. For example, there was an earthquake in Lisbon, Portugal, in 1755. Religious authorities blamed it on sinners instead of nature. Other times, activists spread fake news. They published lies to get people to change their political or religious views.

Some news outlets published fake stories in newspapers long before the internet was around.

FAKE NEWS IN AMERICAN HISTORY

Fake news in the past was often political, just as it is today. Leading up to the American Revolutionary War (1775–1783), people spread propaganda. This is information that is shared to help or hurt certain causes, people, or beliefs. It is usually political. And it is often biased or untrue. Revolutionary leaders spread propaganda. They wanted to increase anti-British feelings. At the time, Britain ruled over the American colonies. Many people there wanted independence. The colonies won the war and became the United States.

Different US newspapers published information for different political parties. Much of what was published was propaganda. Politicians such as Thomas Jefferson claimed that the press often

Thomas Jefferson was the third US president.

published fake news. In 1807, Jefferson was president. He once wrote, "Nothing can now be believed which is seen in a newspaper. Truth itself becomes suspicious by being put into that polluted vehicle."[3]

In the 1830s, printing technology made it possible to print even more newspapers.

Companies sold the papers for very low prices. These factors helped newspapers reach larger audiences. Some newspapers relied on advertising to make money. They published false stories to sell more papers.

The trend of using fake news to make money continued. Yellow journalism became common in the 1890s. This was

THE GREAT MOON HOAX

In 1835, a newspaper published a series of articles filled with fake information. Each talked about new discoveries on the moon. They said plants were growing on the moon and animals lived there. The story also claimed there were winged aliens on the moon. The hoax got many more people to read the newspaper.

exaggerated or fake news that was meant to cause extreme reactions in readers. For example, newspapers used yellow journalism to increase anti-Spanish opinions. A US battleship mysteriously sank in Cuba. Some newspapers blamed the Spanish without evidence. Yellow journalism like this made Americans call for war. It likely contributed to the start of the Spanish–American War (1898).

The influence of yellow journalism also sparked change. People began seeking out accurate and unbiased reporting. The newspaper industry began adopting codes of ethics. Many codes said newspapers should not publish fake or misleading news. Journalism began to improve.

FAKE NEWS IN NAZI GERMANY

Fake news is an issue in other countries as well. In some places, it has come from governments as a tool to control people. Fake news was especially influential in Nazi Germany. Nazi propaganda spread fake news for many years.

In 1919, Nazi leader Adolf Hitler was already beginning his propaganda campaign. He gave speeches spreading horrible and untrue beliefs about Jewish

The Nazis spread anti-Semitic posters as part of their propaganda.

people. Hitler and the Nazi Party started a

newspaper to spread their hateful ideas.

The Nazis assumed power in the

1930s. They took over or destroyed many

publishing companies and newspapers.

They targeted the ones owned by Jewish people or opposing political parties. They also used the radio and news to tell lies that scared people. This allowed the Nazis to make political changes more easily.

FAKE NEWS AS A MILITARY STRATEGY

During World War II (1939–1945), the British government used propaganda in Germany and other countries. It was meant to undermine the Nazis. A man named Denis Sefton Delmer eventually ran the propaganda program. He created radio stations. They spread fake news. On one show, a man pretended he was a German military officer. He told lies designed to make people stop trusting the Nazis. Delmer also produced a newspaper with fake news. It was given to German soldiers. Some soldiers later said they trusted his newspaper more than German news sources.

Nazi propaganda told lies to make people tolerate violence against Jews. It told people that Jews were less than human and that they were enemies of Germany. It tried to hide the horrible treatment of people in concentration camps. The period of time when Germany murdered millions of Jewish people is called the Holocaust.

Many different factors led to the Holocaust. But it is important to recognize how fake news from Nazi authorities contributed to it. It was a strategy for controlling and manipulating people. Other governments throughout history have used fake news to gain and keep power. Some still do it today.

HOW TODAY'S FAKE NEWS STACKS UP

Today, fake news is more common because of the internet and social media. It can spread much more quickly than in the past. Technology such as photo and video editing makes it possible to create different types of fake news. These visuals can make a story even more convincing.

Social media can make people more likely to fall for fake news. It's harder for people to figure out a story's source. When friends and family share a story, the source may be hidden. Social media may also

recommend popular stories to users. But

bots can make these stories seem more

popular than they actually are. All of these

things make fake news today very different

from historical fake news.

PHOTO AND VIDEO EDITING

Fake news can include videos and
photographs. People may share photos with
false captions. They may edit pictures. Doing
this can make it seem like something happened
that did not. Videos may be edited or adjusted
in a way that changes the context. For example,
one video of Democratic politician Nancy Pelosi
was slowed down so she appeared intoxicated.

CHAPTER THREE

WHAT ARE EXAMPLES OF FAKE NEWS?

Many different people create fake news stories. Some say they are writing fake news to make fun of politics. Others say they are trying to show how easily fake news can spread.

There are some fake news writers who claim they are writing satire. A man named

Fake news creators often hide behind computer screens.

Christopher Blair has fake news websites.

He has **disclaimers** on his websites. The disclaimers say the news on the site is not necessarily true. But people share his stories as if they were true anyway.

Some fake news websites don't tell people that their content is made-up.

One famous fake news creator was Paul Horner. In 2016, Donald Trump was running for president. Horner didn't think Trump was a good candidate. Horner wrote stories that many people believed and shared.

For example, many Trump supporters in

the 2016 election didn't believe that people

were really protesting Trump. They thought

these people had been paid to do this.

Horner wrote a story to make fun of this

idea. It said that a Trump protester was paid

$3,500. It wasn't true. But many people

believed the story. Even Trump's campaign

manager shared it on social media.

Fake news writers don't always believe

they have influence. But Horner did worry

about how his work impacted the election.

He said, "My sites were picked up by Trump

supporters all the time. . . . Looking back,

instead of hurting the campaign, I think I

helped it. And that feels [bad]."[4]

HOW COMMON IS FAKE NEWS?

Many people come across fake news. For instance, this happened in 2016. It was before the US presidential election. More than 25 percent of adults went to fake news websites. For a while, fake news seemed more popular than real news. The top twenty fake news stories had more Facebook comments, reactions, and shares than real news stories. Researchers did a survey in 2019. They found that 86 percent of people think they've seen fake news. Most of those people said they believed at least one fake news story when they first saw it.

INTERNATIONAL SOURCES

Some fake news websites that have false information on US politics are run by people in other countries. They copy content from illegitimate US news sources. They try to pass it off as real news.

One group of fake news writers has become especially famous. They've been publishing fake news from Veles, Macedonia, for many years. The unemployment rate is very high in Macedonia. But the creators of the fake news sites made a lot of money from ads. In 2017, the government in Macedonia

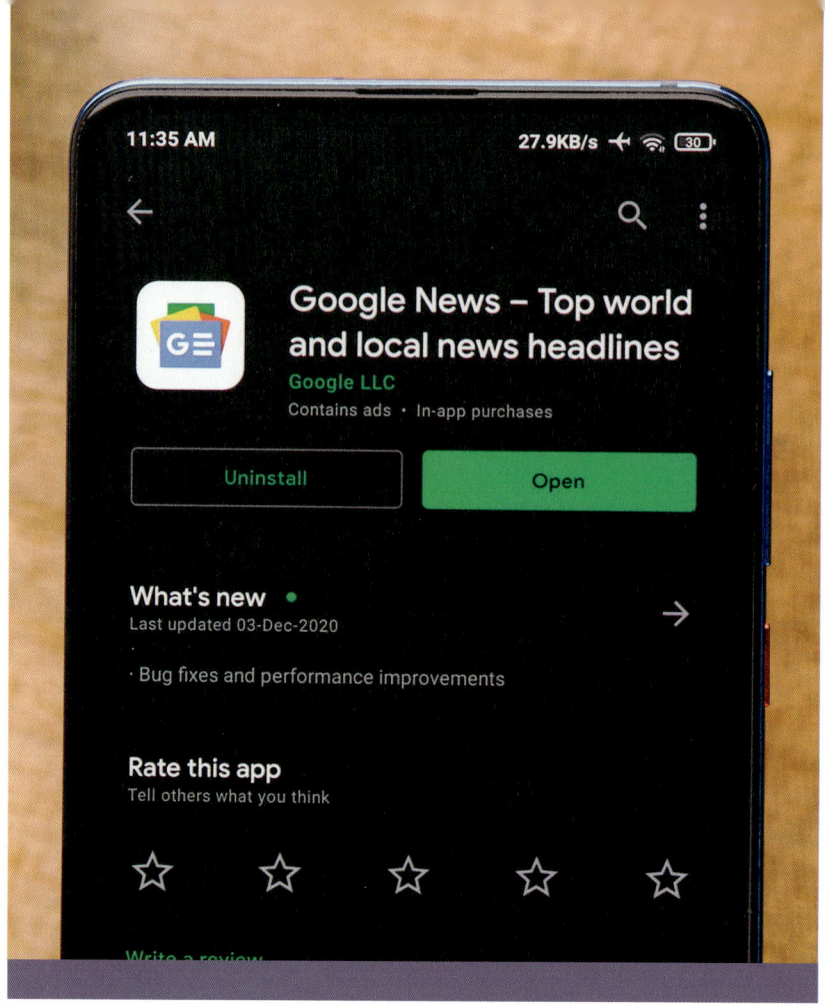

Millions of people get their news through Google.

changed. The new government said it

wanted to reduce fake news. And websites

like Facebook and Google are working

to detect fake news and block it. It has

become harder for the fake news creators

in Macedonia to succeed. But many foreign sites are still spreading fake news.

PIZZAGATE

Some fake news has had serious consequences. One major fake news incident is often called Pizzagate. It took place during the 2016 US presidential election. Hillary Clinton was running against Trump. Shortly before the election, **conspiracy theorists** spread a rumor about a pizza place in Washington, DC. They said that Clinton was helping the owner, James Alefantis, run an operation involving child sexual abuse. There was no evidence for this. The accusation was completely false.

But the story spread on social media. People protested the pizza restaurant. They sent Alefantis and his staff death threats. Edgar Maddison Welch learned about the conspiracy from fake news websites. In December 2016, he went to the restaurant. He brought weapons and fired an assault rifle. Luckily, no one was hurt. But the situation could have led to real injuries or even death.

This incident shows the dangers of fake news. After Welch attacked the restaurant,

Some people went to the White House to try and bring more attention to the Pizzagate conspiracy theory.

Alefantis said, "What happened today demonstrates that promoting false and reckless conspiracy theories comes with consequences. I hope that those involved in fanning these flames will take a moment to contemplate what happened here today, and stop promoting these falsehoods right away."[5] Unfortunately, people still spread conspiracy theories online.

COVID-19

Other fake news stories have led to real-life consequences too. In 2020, there was a great deal of misinformation and fake news about the COVID-19 pandemic. COVID-19 was a disease that spread around the globe. It killed many people. Governments tried to slow the spread. Many banned large gatherings. They asked people to stay away

Wearing face masks in public places helped slow the spread of COVID-19.

from each other. They also wanted people

to wear face masks.

Fake news spread about the pandemic.

Some people said wearing face masks

made people sicker. They claimed powerful

people were using the disease to make

money. They also said a COVID-19 vaccine would kill millions of people. There is no evidence supporting these statements. Because of fake news like this, people believed things that were dangerous to their health. Some people didn't wear masks. Some consumed dangerous chemicals or ineffective drugs. They thought this would protect them from, or even cure, COVID-19. Some people also believed COVID-19 vaccines were unsafe.

A lot of the fake news was politically motivated. In one case, a photograph of Democratic lawmakers was shared

Some fake news stories told people to drink disinfectant to help with COVID-19.

online. They were not wearing masks.

It was published in fake news articles

vaguely suggesting a conspiracy. But the

photograph was taken in 2019. That was

before COVID-19 cases were confirmed

in the United States. There were no rules about wearing masks at the time.

THE CAPITOL RIOT

In January 2021, a group of people gathered outside the US Capitol in Washington, DC. Congress was in session. Lawmakers were certifying the 2020 presidential election results. They were confirming that Joe Biden won the election against President Trump.

For many weeks before this, fake news about the election spread. It claimed that the election results weren't accurate. Some of the false information came from Trump

The Capitol riot cost the country more than $30 million in damages and security expenses.

and other government leaders. Trump said

the election had been stolen from him.

These claims were not true. Investigations

and recounts took place. No evidence

was found to overturn the election in

Trump's favor.

Trump encouraged his supporters to go to the US Capitol building to stop the election results from getting certified. Many did. The supporters began rioting. They got onto the Capitol grounds. They fought

JOURNALISTS HARASSED

People who disagree with a news story may call it fake. This has real consequences for people, especially journalists. During the Capitol riot, Trump supporters harassed journalists. They destroyed journalists' equipment. They shouted that the media was the enemy of the people. This is something Trump had said before. Politicians sometimes call legitimate news sources fake. Many people believe this has contributed to harassment and violence against journalists.

with police officers and eventually got into the building. Lawmakers had to flee. Many feared for their lives. Five people died during the riot, including a police officer and four Trump supporters.

Fake news takes many forms. It can come from a variety of sources, including elected officials and other leaders. It can have very serious and even deadly consequences. This is one reason why it's important to identify fake news.

CHAPTER FOUR

HOW CAN I IDENTIFY FAKE NEWS?

There are many techniques to recognize fake news. One of the most important ways to check if something is fake news is to look at the source. Is the article from a **reputable** publication? People can look for suspicious URLs. Sometimes fake news websites try to look just like trusted news

Taking a close look at news sources can help people identify fake stories.

sources. They may have ".co" at the end.

One fake news site posed as ABC News.

Its URL was abcnews.com.co. But the real

ABC News website is abcnews.go.com.

People can put the name of a trusted

news source into a search engine, such as

Google. They can see if the URL they find

in the search engine matches the one from
the article.

MORE RESEARCH

If people don't recognize the source as
trustworthy, they should do more research.
One way to do this is with the "About"
section on a website. This section has
information about the website and the
people behind it. It is likely a sign of fake
news if there is no "About" page or if the
site asks people to register in order to find
out more. "About" pages may also help
identify satire. Some sites will clearly state
that their content is satirical. Others may

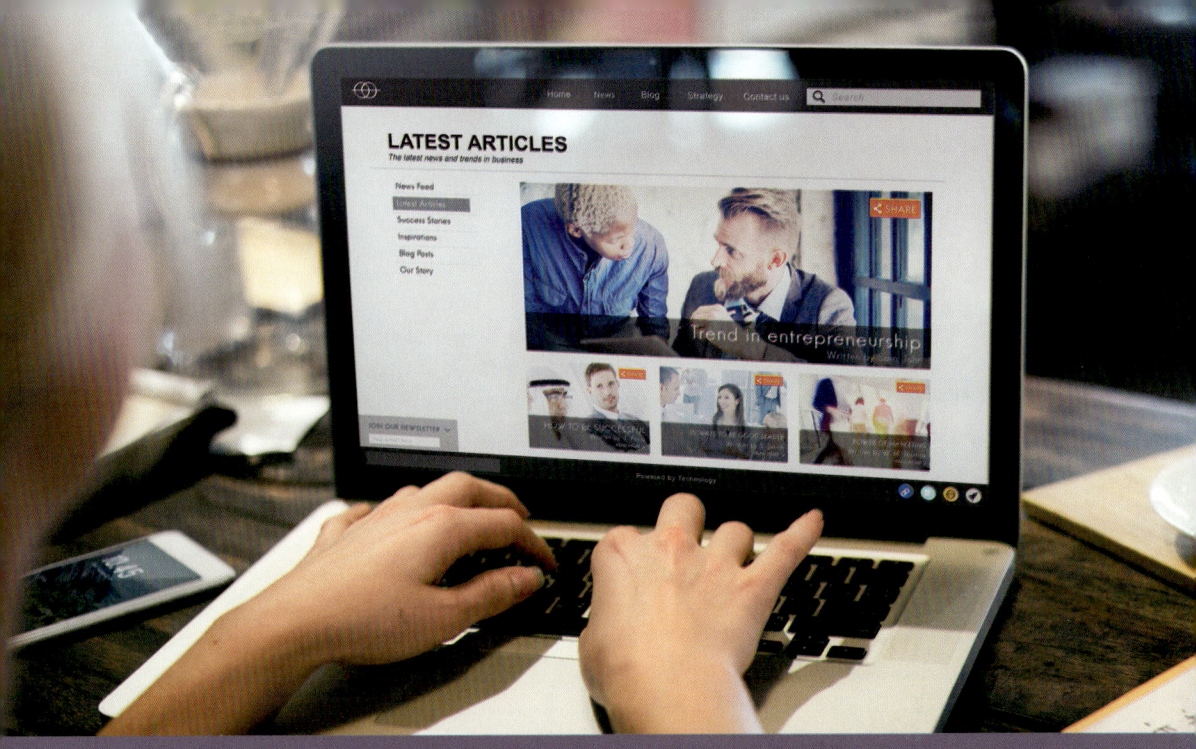

Searching through a source's website may give people insight into whether they should trust it.

use jokes to show the site does not publish real news. Still, not everyone understands that these are jokes.

The "Contact" page is another good place to check. Sources without contact information may be suspicious. People can also look at other news stories posted on

With good media literacy skills, people will be less likely to believe fake information.

the site. The stories may be very obviously false or dramatic. This tells people that the site doesn't always post credible news.

CHECK THE STYLE AND THE STORY

Some fake news sources can be easily spotted. The stories may have strange formatting. For instance, some words may be bold or in all caps. The layout may be awkward too. The stories may have major grammatical or spelling errors.

It can also help to look at the ads on a page. Some real news sources have ads, so this shouldn't be the only clue to identify an unreliable website. But fake news sources often have many ads. These include pop-up ads. Ads on fake news sites are often inappropriate. They may use sex appeal to get readers to click.

There may be many clues within a fake news story beyond grammar and formatting. One thing to check is the date. Old fake news stories may spread again. Dates within the story may be suspicious as well. Timelines within stories may not make sense. Or dates of real events may be wrong.

Checking the author's sources is important. A story may quote experts without giving names. It may cite laws or studies that don't actually reflect what the story claims. It may even cite completely made-up sources. For example, stories could mention studies from organizations that don't exist. Some stories may not

Reputable journalists try to report stories without bias.

provide any evidence at all. Looking for

links can also give people clues about how

legitimate the stories are. For instance,

stories may link to illegitimate sources.

Or they may not have any links. This may be a sign that the stories are fake.

The story's photos can provide clues too. Many fake news stories use photos that have been manipulated. Some may include real pictures. But these photos are paired with text that takes them out of context. A reverse photo search may help people detect photo misuse or alteration.

One reliable way to check a story is to search the claim online. The story may have been debunked by fact-checking websites. Or the story may not be covered by any reputable news sources.

People use photo editing software to manipulate images.

A strong emotional reaction to a headline or story can be a sign that the news is fake. People should consider their reactions while reading. If they feel very angry or very smug, this can be a sign of fake news. People should always consider their own biases.

They should question whether they believe something simply because it supports their opinions.

RESPONDING TO FAKE NEWS

People are taking steps to help prevent the spread of fake news. Some social media platforms mark fake news stories when they find them. Many also have ways for users to flag these stories. However, there are some drawbacks to this. Some people believe that social media platforms are perfect at identifying fake news. They think that any story that isn't marked as fake must be real. This is not the case.

An associate professor named David Rand led a study on Facebook's fact-checking feature. The study found that people were more likely to share unmarked fake news when only some of the fake news stories on the platform were marked as fake.

ARTIFICIAL INTELLIGENCE

Researchers want to use artificial intelligence to find fake news. They've taught software to look for certain signs. It looks at the sentence structure of headlines. It also looks at the kinds of words used in articles. The software also looks at the source's URL. It analyzes website traffic, social media usage, and more. Some software can find fake news more than 90 percent of the time.

Rand explained, "When you start putting warning labels on some things, it makes everything else seem more credible."[6]

There are many ways people can identify fake news. They can also help fight the spread of fake news. People shouldn't share news if they're not sure it's real. They can flag fake news on social media. They can leave a comment on the post and let others know that the story is fake. Fake news has real-world consequences. But savvy media consumers can make sure fake news doesn't inform their opinions or beliefs.

GLOSSARY

biases

prejudices that influence one's opinions and beliefs, sometimes unfairly

conspiracy theorists

people who believe in conspiracy theories, which are beliefs that certain events are secretly planned by powerful people or organizations

credible

trustworthy or believable

disclaimers

statements that clarify something is not true or that one is not legally responsible for something

parody

to imitate or exaggerate something in order to make fun of it

reputable

widely believed to be trustworthy or of good quality

satire

a type of humor that uses irony or sarcasm to criticize or make a point about something, such as politics

verified

confirmed something or made sure it is true

SOURCE NOTES

CHAPTER ONE: WHAT IS FAKE NEWS?

1. Quoted in Laura Sydell, "We Tracked Down a Fake-News Creator in the Suburbs. Here's What We Learned," *NPR*, November 23, 2016. www.npr.org.

2. Quoted in "Fake News Expert on How False Stories Spread and Why People Believe Them," *NPR*, December 14, 2016. www.npr.org.

CHAPTER TWO: WHAT IS THE HISTORY OF FAKE NEWS?

3. Quoted in David Uberti, "The Real History of Fake News," *Columbia Journalism Review*, December 15, 2016. www.cjr.org.

CHAPTER THREE: WHAT ARE EXAMPLES OF FAKE NEWS?

4. Quoted in Caitlin Dewey, "Facebook Fake-News Writer: 'I Think Donald Trump Is in the White House Because of Me,'" *Washington Post*, November 17, 2016. www.washingtonpost.com.

5. Quoted in "Comet Ping Pong," *Facebook*, December 4, 2016. www.facebook.com.

CHAPTER FOUR: HOW CAN I IDENTIFY FAKE NEWS?

6. Quoted in Mark Wilson, "Study: Facebook's Fake News Labels Have a Fatal Flaw," *Fast Company*, March 4, 2020. www.fastcompany.com.

FOR FURTHER RESEARCH

BOOKS

Kari A. Cornell, *Fake News*. San Diego, CA: BrightPoint Press, 2020.

Pamela Dell, *Understanding the News.* North Mankato, MN: Capstone Press, 2019.

Lisa A. McPartland, *The Importance of Good Sources*. New York: PowerKids Press, 2019.

INTERNET SOURCES

"How to Be an Expert Fact-Checker," *National Geographic Kids*, n.d. https://kids.nationalgeographic.com.

Lina Mai, "Making Sense of the Media," *Time for Kids*, September 7, 2018. www.timeforkids.com.

"What Is Fake News?" *Wonderopolis*, n.d. https://wonderopolis.org.

WEBSITES

Crash Course
https://thecrashcourse.com

Crash Course has a collection of videos to help viewers evaluate, use, and interpret information from different news sources. Viewers can explore the courses in the Navigating Digital Information and Media Literacy sections to learn more.

News Literacy Project: News Literacy Tips & Tools
https://newslit.org/tips-tools

This collection of articles, quizzes, and more comes from the News Literacy Project, a nonprofit dedicated to educating people on consuming news wisely.

PBS Learning Media News and Media Literacy Collection: Fake News
https://tpt.pbslearningmedia.org/collection/fake-news

This collection of resources includes videos and handouts to help users identify and understand fake news.

INDEX

IMAGE CREDITS

ABOUT THE AUTHOR

R. L. Van is a writer and editor living in Minnesota. She has written nonfiction books for kids and teens on a variety of topics. In her free time, she enjoys reading, doing crossword puzzles, and caring for her pet cats.